My Blanket

For Ashley

18375352

VIKING KESTREL

Viking Penguin Inc., 40 West 23rd Street, New York, New York 10010, U.S.A.
Penguin Books Ltd, Harmondsworth, Middlesex, England
Penguin Books Australia Ltd, Ringwood, Victoria, Australia
Penguin Books Canada Limited, 2801 John Street, Markham, Ontario, Canada L3R 1B4
Penguin Books (N.Z.) Ltd, 182–190 Wairau Road, Auckland 10, New Zealand

Copyright © Ruth Young, 1987
All rights reserved

First published in 1987 by Viking Penguin Inc.
Published simultaneously in Canada

Manufactured in Singapore by Imago Publishing Ltd.
Set in Garamond #3

1   2   3   4   5   91   90   89   88   87

Library of Congress Cataloging in Publication Data
Young, Ruth, 1946–   My blanket.
Summary: A toddler's blue blanket goes with him everywhere.
[1. Blankets—Fiction]   I. Title.   PZ7.Y877Mz   1987   [E]   87-6282   ISBN 0-670-81306-0

My Blanket

"Me and Silkie"

RUTH YOUNG

VIKING KESTREL

Do you have a special blanket?
I do. I call it Silkie.

Silkie is like a blanket,
only more than a blanket.

It helps me go to sleep,

Or helps me feel better
if I have a bad dream.

The first time we washed Silkie,
Silkie came out much littler.

But soon it almost felt the same.

It is nice to have along on trips,

Or visiting a friend.

I like to take it everywhere.

Daddy had a Silkie when he was very little. He called it Binkie.

He does not know where Binkie is now.
He says he does not need it anymore.

Silkie is blue and soft, soft, soft.

What color is your blanket?

3